CONTENTS

❦ Lake Classic Short Stories ❧

"The universe is made of stories, not atoms."
—Muriel Rukeyser

"The story's about you."
—Horace

Everyone loves a good story. It is hard to think of a friendlier introduction to classic literature. For one thing, short stories are *short*—quick to get into and easy to finish. Of all the literary forms, the short story is the least intimidating and the most approachable.

Great literature is an important part of our human heritage. In the belief that this heritage belongs to everyone, *Lake Classic Short Stories* are adapted for today's readers. Lengthy sentences and paragraphs are shortened. Archaic words are replaced. Modern punctuation and spellings are used. Many of the longer stories are abridged. In all the stories,

5

painstaking care has been taken to preserve the author's unique voice.

Lake Classic Short Stories have something for everyone. The hundreds of stories in the collection cover a broad terrain of themes, story types, and styles. Literary merit was a deciding factor in story selection. But no story was included unless it was as enjoyable as it was instructive. And special priority was given to stories that shine light on the human condition.

Each book in the *Lake Classic Short Stories* is devoted to the work of a single author. Little-known stories of merit are included with famous old favorites. Taken as a whole, the collected authors and stories make up a rich and diverse sampler of the story-teller's art.

Lake Classic Short Stories guarantee a great reading experience. Readers who look for common interests, concerns, and experiences are sure to find them. Readers who bring their own gifts of perception and appreciation to the stories will be doubly rewarded.

❦ Irvin S. Cobb ❧
(1876–1944)

About the Author

Irvin Shrewsbury Cobb could trace his family tree back to the earliest settlers of the state of Kentucky. He began high school in his home town of Paducah, but dropped out after two years. At 15, he was driving an ice wagon, collecting for newspapers, and delivering flyers. He was also selling a few cartoons to local papers and making plans to become a cartoonist.

At 16, Cobb got a job as a cub reporter on the local newspaper. His career as a writer had begun. By the time he was 19, he was the paper's managing editor— the youngest managing editor in the United States at that time.

Cobb worked as a journalist for many years. He wrote for the *New York Sun* and the *World*, the *Saturday Evening Post*, and for *Cosmopolitan*.

"I didn't write my first short story until I was in my 37th year," Cobb explained, ". . . an age when many short story writers have written themselves out."

In the years that followed, Cobb wrote a huge number of books and stories. His forthright American humor has been compared to that of Mark Twain. He once explained that his "preference" had always been for "simple people and commonplace things."

In his later years, Cobb and his wife moved from New York to Santa Monica, California. There he tried his hand at writing movie scripts. When he was nearly 60, he even acted in a few films. "I never had any trouble controlling my fan mail," Cobb wrote. In the end he would not be remembered as a screen star but as a humorist and a storyteller.

Five Hundred Dollars Reward

The family feud had been going on for 20 years. Why didn't old Rance Fleming simply keep his distance from young Jim Faxon? But it didn't work out that way. Now Judge Priest has to figure out a way to make things right.

"I WANTED TO SEE IF YOU'RE LIKE THE REST OF THE
CHICKEN-HEARTED FAXONS. I GUESS YOU ARE."

Five Hundred Dollars Reward

There was once a feud down in our part of Kentucky. It wasn't one of those bloody feuds of the mountains. It didn't involve a whole district. It didn't force an enlargement of the cemetery.

It was a small, neighborhood feud. Only two families were involved—the Flemings and the Faxons. Still, such as it was, this feud lasted off and on for 20 years or more.

It started with an argument over a property line. This was back during the Civil War. What happened was this: A Faxon shot a Fleming. Then the Faxon was in turn shot by one of the Flemings. And so it went. Finally most of the Faxons got tired of it all and moved to Tennessee. One branch of them came into our town and settled here.

As time went by, the feud became mostly a memory. It came alive for a while, though. That happened when old Rance Fleming was killed by young Jim Faxon. It was then the feud died, and died for good.

By all accounts the Faxons fought mostly in self-defense. They lacked the meanness of the Flemings. And one of the meanest of all was old Rance Fleming.

I remember how we boys used to watch him, when he came to town. Old Rance was always unshaven and dirty. Often he was half drunk. Late in the afternoon he would get in his wagon and head home. He'd whip his poor old horses until they danced with terror.

At night the older men would tell stories about him. They talked of the war years. Back then old Rance had been a raider. He was loyal to neither the North nor the South. He'd attack first on one side and then on the other. He'd steal whatever he could, and then try to burn the rest.

Young Jim Faxon was a different kind of person altogether. He was a small, quiet, decent young fellow. He minded his own business. He worked hard keeping a vegetable stand at the town market.

Young Jim lived with his aunt, old Miss Whitley. He was her main source of support. The rumor was that young Jim was saving his money. When he was old enough, and had enough money saved, he planned to marry the Hardin girl.

Emmy Hardin was Jim's distant cousin. She was also an orphan. She too lived with Miss Whitley. Sometimes in good weather she'd come to town with Jim and help out at the vegetable stand. She was a pretty little thing, and shy as a bunny.

During his early years, young Jim had no trouble with the Flemings. Perhaps old Rance thought the boy was not worth the attention of giving him an insult.

But just after Jim had turned 20, everything changed. Without warning, Rance Fleming set out to pick a fight with him. It was as awful as anything could be. Suddenly, Rance's hidden hate came rushing up from deep inside him.

One Saturday afternoon in November, Rance came into town. Saturday was always a busy day in town. The market was set up in an old building with a sagging roof. It was closed in the middle and open at the ends. There were giant cracks in the side walls.

Besides vegetables, people sold fruit, fresh fish, and meat there. The country boys and girls were poor. They searched the woods and the fields for something to sell. Sometimes they would bring in quail, rabbit, and possum. You might also find wild grapes, hickory nuts, and blueberries there, too.

As I was saying, it was on a Saturday in November when the trouble started. Rance Fleming decided to shame Jim Faxon in front of the crowd. You could tell by his look what he was up to. He had been drinking that day and was a bit shaky in his walk. When he got to the Faxon stall, he just stood there. He stuck his head forward and spread his legs apart. Then he just stared hard into young Jim's face.

Everybody in that end of the market could tell what was coming. Both sellers and buyers turned around to see what would happen. Those in the rear stood on their tiptoes. Some people climbed onto the wagons that were backed up in rows alongside the open shed. The silence grew electric.

Young Jim wanted no trouble. That was plain enough to see. He seemed at a loss for words. He turned his face away from the glare of the old man. He pretended to straighten out the rows of vegetables on the table.

Poor Jim's hands were trembling. They trembled so much he overturned a bowl of dried peas. The peas rolled to the edge of the table. Then they fell, spattering off in a steady stream. The back of the boy's neck turned a dark red. Those who looked on felt sorry for him. He seemed so young and helpless. Most of the people felt glad that Jim's girl, little Emmy Hardin, wasn't there.

Old Rance just stood there without saying a word. He was enjoying young Faxon's embarrassment. When he did speak, he talked as though he had sand in his mouth.

"Look here, you," he said.

Jim lifted his head. "Mister Fleming," he answered. "What—what is it you want with me—Mister Fleming?"

"Mister Fleming—Mister Fleming," the older man said in a mocking voice. "*Mister* Fleming, huh? Well, you know mighty good and well what I want with you. I want to see if you're as white-livered as the rest of the chicken-hearted Faxons used to be. And I guess you are.

"*Mister* Fleming, huh?" the old man went on. "Well, from now on that's what you'd *better* call me. The next time I come by, you'd better take off your hat to me, too. Do you hear me? You—!"

Fleming called Jim a terrible name. It was a fighting word, even worse than throwing a punch.

The people watching stepped back a little. They thought for sure that Jim would attack old Rance. But there was no forward rush by the younger man. Young Jim Faxon just stood and took it without a word or an action.

Old Rance looked at him and laughed with scorn. Then he turned around and walked off. He didn't look back, either. It was clear that he thought Jim was too cowardly to come after him.

The whole thing took less than a minute. The last of the spilled peas were still falling off the table. Young Jim stood with his head hanging on his chest. He looked straight down at the table. He couldn't face any of the people standing near him.

* * *

People talked about it all that night and for days after. It was not an easy thing to forget. A grown man was too scared to stand up to an insult! A fistfight might have been forgotten. Even a fistfight between a Faxon and a Fleming. But not this.

Some people didn't see how Jim could ever hold his head up again. And he didn't hold his head up. At least he didn't hold it as high as he used to. He had always been a quiet young man. Now he was almost mute.

More than a month went by. Old Rance didn't come to town until the Saturday just before Christmas. On that day the Christmas feeling was in the air. The market was the busiest place in town. Little Emmy Hardin was helping Jim at the stand. As she worked, she kept giving him loving looks.

Then Rance Fleming showed up. He elbowed his way through the crowd. His face was red with temper—and whiskey. His cotton shirt was open at the throat so that his hairy chest showed. His pants were splashed with mud. He wore neither a coat nor a vest. He had a dirty overcoat swung over his shoulders. Its arms were tied loosely around his neck.

Before young Jim or Emmy saw him, he was right upon them. Only the vegetable table separated them. Without warning, Fleming leaned across the table and called Jim the terrible name he'd called him before. Then he slapped Jim in the face with his open hand.

The boy pulled back from the blow. Only the ends of Rance's fingers touched his cheek. But that was enough. Jim had been slapped in the face—right before the eyes of his sweetheart!

The young girl gasped. She tried to put her arms about young Jim, but he shooed her off.

Old Rance was pleased with his work. He started to back away, all the time watching young Jim. People stepped out of Rance's way. When he was clear of the market shed, he turned his back to Jim. Then he headed for one of the saloons across the street.

There was a pawn shop next door. Some folks called it the "pistol store" because the owner always displayed revolvers in the front window.

The crowd watched as old Rance went into the saloon. When they looked back toward the Faxon's stall, Jim was gone. He had vanished without a word. Emmy Hardin was alone. Her face was buried in her arms. She sobbed as though she would never stop. Then she turned and ran off.

"Oh, dear. Now there's liable to be trouble," an old woman said.

"I reckon not," said a man nearby. "It looks to me like Jim Faxon is plain afraid. It looks like he ain't got the spirit of a rabbit left in him."

Because she had hurried off, Emmy Hardin was spared the sight of what followed.

Old Rance had one drink in the first saloon. Then he came out and headed for the next saloon along the row.

Then, as he passed the pawn shop, he heard a shout behind him. Young Jim Faxon was stepping out of the "pistol store." Tears were streaming down his face. His right arm was down at his side. His hand was clutching a pistol.

Old Rance made no move toward his own hip pocket. We found out later that he wasn't even carrying a pen-knife. In surprise, he stepped backwards, with his hands raised. Before he had gone three steps, young Jim brought the pistol up. He fired just once. But once was enough.

Old Rance fell forward. Two men ran to him and turned him over on his back. For a moment, young Jim just stood there, looking at what he'd done. Then he stopped crying and dropped the pistol on the sidewalk.

Next a police officer appeared. He spoke to one of the people standing nearby. Then he went over to Jim Faxon and arrested him. He started to put handcuffs on the boy.

"You don't need to be putting those things on me," said Jim. "I'll go along with you, all right. It's all over now— *everything's* over!"

* * *

The sympathy of the town was with young Jim. But the law of the land was dead set against him on all counts.

He had not fired his gun in sudden heat and passion. He had taken time to go and buy a gun. The insult from Fleming had been great, but he could not claim self-defense. Everyone knew that old Rance had meant to start trouble. Still, he was backing off at the moment Jim shot him.

Jim Faxon was caught in the web of the law. Many local people offered to put up bail for him. It made no difference. Bail wasn't allowed for murder cases in our county. So Jim was put in the county jail. And there he would stay until the circuit court opened its doors the following spring.

Nobody believed that a jury would vote for the death sentence. The dead man's intentions and his evil reputation were well known. Taken with Jim's good reputation, that put things in the young man's favor.

Still, it was generally believed Jim would be found guilty of manslaughter. He might get four years in prison for killing old Rance. Or six years—or even ten. There seemed to be no way out of it. People felt sorrier than ever for Jim. Not to mention for his aunt and for Emmy.

Jim's aunt put a mortgage of five hundred dollars on her house. With that money, she hired Dabney Prentiss, the best lawyer in the county.

On the evening before the trial began, Judge William Pitman Priest sat on his porch. He was alone, enjoying the spring weather. It was getting dark when he heard the front gate open. He looked down the path and saw two women coming toward him. They were Miss Whitley and little Emmy Hardin.

The judge said, "Howdy, Miss Whitley. Emmy, child, how are you? Well, come on in. Set down and rest yourselves."

"Judge Priest, we've come about my nephew Jimmy," Miss Whitley said.

Judge Priest was alarmed. "Did Mister Dabney Prentiss—did *anyone*—send you here to see me on this business?" he asked.

"No, sir, nobody at all," answered the old woman. "We just came on our own.

We felt we just *had* to come and see you. Oh, Judge Priest, we are in so much trouble, Emmy and me. We need your help."

The judge raised his hand, as though to stop her. But the old woman was not to be stopped.

"Judge Priest, you've known me these many years," she said. "And you know how it was in them old days. The Flemings were forever fighting with my people and forcing trouble on us. And you know Jimmy, too. You know how he's always stood by me and helped me out, just like a son. And I guess you know about him and Emmy here." She broke off to wipe her eyes.

"Miss Whitley, I'm sorry," Judge Priest said very softly. "But it isn't proper for the judge in a case to discuss his feelings about it. I can't talk about the case with you now. I'm sorry—but that's the law."

"The law!" she cried out. "Where was the law when Rance Fleming was pushing Jimmy into a fight? Fleming was a cruel, swearing, drunken bully. He

forced Jimmy to do what he did. Now what kind of law will send that boy to prison?" She looked at Emmy. "And what about this poor child?"

"Madame," said the Judge kindly. "It's not for me to discuss these matters with you now. It's not even proper that I should let you say these things to me."

"Oh, but Judge," she said. "You *must* listen to me. When Rance first insulted Jimmy, we begged him not to fight. Jimmy promised that he wouldn't. But Rance wouldn't let him alone. After he slapped Jimmy's face, Jimmy knew what was coming. Sooner or later, he knew he'd have to kill Rance Fleming—or be killed himself."

Judge Priest cleared his throat. "Miss Whitley, your nephew will have a fair trial. I promise you that. But that is all I can say to you now."

Shaking her head, the old woman turned away.

"Just one minute, please, Miss Whitley," said Judge Priest. "I'd like to ask you a question. Is it true what I hear?

Have you mortgaged your house to raise the money for this boy's defense?"

"Yes, sir," she answered. "It's true. But please don't let Jimmy know. He thinks I had the money saved up from the market. No matter how his case goes, I don't ever want him to know."

She paused for just a moment. Then a flash of fire came into her eyes.

"Judge Priest, that Rance Fleming *deserved* killing. You were off in the army during the Big War. Maybe you don't remember when Rance Fleming was a raider. He went back and forth along the state line here. He burned houses and mistreated women and children. I tell you, there were soldiers out after him. They had orders to shoot him down on sight. After the terrible things he did, he didn't have any right to live!"

"Come, we'd better be going," said Emmy, taking her aunt's arm.

Then the two women said goodnight to Judge Priest and headed home. After they left, the judge reached for his hat and started down the pathway.

* * *

Half an hour later, there were lights shining from two big windows in the courthouse. The light came from Judge Priest's office. Inside, the judge was looking through big stacks of legal records. Some of them were dusty and torn with age. Finally, after several hours, he got up from his desk. He'd found what he wanted.

* * *

The next morning, young Jim Faxon's case was called. When the jailer brought him in, Jim was wearing handcuffs. Then the jailer realized he'd forgotten the key, so he hurried back to the jail to find it. Jim sat between his women folk. Emmy Hardin put her small hands over the steel cuffs. She meant to hide the shameful sight from the eyes of the crowd. She kept her hands there until the jailer came back and unlocked the handcuffs.

This little group of three sat there silently and pale-faced just inside the rail. In front of them stood Jim Faxon's lawyer, Dabney Prentiss.

The case was called right away. Both sides—the defense and the prosecution—announced they were ready to proceed to trial. The crowd sat forward to watch the choosing of the jurors. But there were never to be any jurors picked.

Judge Priest cleared his throat. Then he spoke.

"Before we proceed—" he began. His tone clearly showed that what he was about to say would be well worth hearing. "Before we proceed, I have something important to say. It has a direct bearing on the case."

He glanced about him silently, commanding quiet.

"The defendant is charged with the death of Ransom Fleming," the judge went on.

He lifted an old piece of folded paper from the desk.

"This record goes back to the last days of the Civil War. It seems that in 1865, Ransom Fleming was a fugitive from justice. He was charged with some serious crimes—burning houses, stealing property, and trying to kill both women and children. But while the war was on, there were no police to bring Fleming to justice. Because of that, the governor of this state took the following action: He offered a reward of $500 for the capture of Ransom Fleming—dead or alive."

Now, everyone there in the crowded courtroom snapped to attention.

"Here in my hand I hold an official copy of the governor's order," continued Judge Priest. "It urges all law-abiding persons to capture Ransom Fleming."

Judge Priest's voice began to rise now. "This order was never withdrawn. It was in full force when James Faxon shot and killed Ransom Fleming. Because of that, James Faxon cannot be charged with a crime. So I now declare him a free man."

At that, the crowd broke out in wild cheering. Anyone in the street outside might have thought a riot was going on. Young Jim Faxon took Emmy and his aunt in his arms. Both women burst out in tears of joy.

The Judge picked up his gavel and pounded for order. In a few minutes the courtroom was quiet again.

"As I was saying—the defendant is a free man," said Judge Priest. "He is also entitled to the $500 reward. That was the amount placed upon the late Ransom Fleming's head by the governor of Kentucky."

Young Jim Faxon cried out, "No, Judge, please, sir! I couldn't touch that money—"

Judge Priest stopped him. "You are not yet of legal age," the judge said. "So I order that this reward be turned over to your legal guardian. It may be that she will find a good use for it."

This time, the cheering was even louder than it had been before. But the judge didn't bother to pound his gavel. He had turned to shake hands with the Attorney for the Defense, Dabney Prentiss.

Words and
Music

Breck Tandy made a big mistake when he killed the most popular man in town. How could he possibly get a fair trial? Things were looking pretty bad for Breck—until Judge Priest remembered seeing that traveling musician.

THE TRAVELING MUSICIAN COULD PLAY ALMOST ANY
TUNE YOU WANTED.

Words and Music

When Breck Tandy killed the man, he made a number of mistakes. First, Tandy killed the most popular man in Forked Deer County, Tennessee. He killed Abner Rankin, the county clerk. Second, he killed him with no witnesses present. Tandy was a newcomer to town and a stranger. So it was his word against the silent accusation of the dead man. Third, Tandy sent to Indiana for a lawyer to defend him.

On the first Monday in June the town square filled up early. That day—Court Monday—the county court opened its session. By nine o'clock the farmers had brought their goods to town. The horse traders were already doing business.

A tall young black man sat tipped back in his chair in front of the Drummers' Home Hotel. He was a traveling musician who played a harmonica. He used his left hand to slide it back and forth across his lips. In the other hand he held a pair of polished beef bones. Around his wrist was a leather strap with three big sleigh-bells attached. He could clap the bones and shake the bells with the same motion. The man was a whole orchestra in himself. He could play almost any tune you wanted. Together, the bones, bells, and harmonica made him sound like a fife-and-drum corps.

The town marshal walked up and down the street. He wore a blue vest over his shirt. A shiny silver shield was pinned to it. High up on the courthouse roof, a red-headed woodpecker tried to drill through the tin covering. Other birds called to one another in the trees around the red-brick building.

Then at ten o'clock, when the sun was high and hot, the sheriff came out of the courthouse. He announced that the trial of Breck Tandy was about to start. Tandy was charged with murder in the first degree. The public announcement was mostly for form, though. Everybody involved in the case was already inside the courthouse.

The air inside the crowded chamber was already hot and sticky. Men were perched on the ledges of the windowsills. More men were ranged in rows along the plastered walls. The two front benches were full of women. This was going to be the biggest case of the June term.

The prisoner sat up front. He had already spent three months in the county jail, and he looked pale. He was tall and steady-eyed, a young man well under age 30. It seemed that he was paying no attention to those who sat in packed rows behind him. He kept his head turned straight ahead. Sometimes he bent down to whisper to one of his lawyers or one of his witnesses. Often his hand went out toward his wife. He would touch her hair, or rest it for a moment on her small shoulder.

Mrs. Tandy was a plain-looking, scared little thing. She was already trembling. Once in a while she would raise her face. Then her brown eyes showed her fear. But quickly she would sink her head back down again, like a quail trying to hide. No one could look more sad and lonely.

Mr. Durham was the chief attorney for the defense. He sat half turned away from the small counsel table. He studied the faces of the crowd. Mr. Durham was from Indiana. He was widely known as a very good lawyer. He had taken on many difficult cases and won them all. But he didn't like what he saw today as he studied the packed courtroom.

Wherever he looked, he saw no friendliness. None at all. He could feel that the crowd was dead set against the man he was defending. And he guessed that the one person *most* against him was Aunt Tilly Haslett. She sat on the very front bench. Because she was a big woman, her husband, Uncle Fayette, was half hidden behind her.

Aunt Tilly was well-known in town. She made public opinion in Hyattsville. Indeed she *was* public opinion in that town. As she sat, she fanned herself with a palm leaf fan. The fan had an edging of black tape sewed around it. Her little gray eyes glared at the strange lawyer. Peering out of her steel-rimmed glasses, she glared at the defendant and his young little wife, too.

Attorney Durham guessed how Aunt Tilly felt about him. She probably thought his tie was too bright. His silk shirt and fancy suit probably bothered her, too. And she probably didn't like it that he came from a northern state. He realized now more than ever how hard his job would be. He feared what was coming—as much for himself as for the man he was defending. But Attorney Durham was a trained veteran of courtroom battles. He tried to put up a good front. Trying not to show his doubts, he made a lively show of talking with the local attorney who would help him in the trial.

The prosecutor was State's Attorney Thomas Gilliam. He showed *real* confidence. He felt certain he could prove that the defendant was guilty. Rankin, the dead man, had been a bachelor. So Gilliam couldn't bring in a widow and orphans to get the jury's sympathy. But the dead man's two sisters were in court. They were thin old women, all dressed in black. They wore veils over their faces. When the right time came, Gilliam would have them raise their veils. Then the jury would see the pitiful sadness in their tired faces.

Attorney Gilliam was a tall, thin man with a little white beard. He was not much of a speaker, but he was a mighty cross-examiner. Today he wore a long black coat and a white vest. His gray striped trousers were just a little bit too short for him.

"Look yonder at Tom Gilliam." Mr. Lukins, a grocer, was speaking to the man sitting next to him. "He sure looks ready to get at that there Tandy and his fancy dude Yankee lawyer. If he don't chew both of them up together, I'll be surprised."

"You bet," his neighbor whispered back. It was Aunt Tilly's oldest son, Fayette, Jr. "It's like Maw says—it's time to teach them Kentuckians a lesson. They can't come down here and kill people and not pay for it."

Just then the judge came in. He was an older, kindly-looking man. The court clerk was right behind him, carrying a large leather-covered book and thick stacks of paper. Aunt Tilly looked straight ahead and squared herself away. This forced Uncle Fayette to lean forward and peek around her.

The prisoner raised his head and eyed the judge. His wife looked only at her hands, which were tightly gripped together. Then the clerk said the case of the State of Tennessee against Tandy was about to begin. Both sides were ready. First off, the accused man pleaded

not guilty. Then the task of picking the
jurors began.

* * *

In an hour the jury was complete. Two
men from town and ten men from the
country were picked. Most of the men
were farmers. But there were also a
clerk, a telegraph operator, a blacksmith,
and a horse-trader. The foreman of the
jury was a tanned old man who looked
like a hawk. He had hands like claws.

It was late in the afternoon when the
prosecution rested its case. Then the
court adjourned until the following
morning.

The prosecutor, Attorney Gilliam, did
not have much evidence to offer. First
there was a statement from the person
who heard the shot and ran into Rankin's
office. He said he had found Rankin lying
dead on the floor with a pistol in his
hand. The pistol had not been fired. He
said he saw Tandy standing there, too.
He also had a pistol in his hand. But his
pistol *had* been fired.

Then there were statements from

persons who knew of a quarrel between Tandy and Rankin. It had to do with a business deal that had gone wrong. It seemed that the two men had once been partners.

While he was examining a witness, Gilliam let his eyes fall on the dead man's two sisters. As he did, they both raised their veils. For a moment, Gilliam stopped talking. He pretended to be overcome with grief at the sight of them. It was an old trick—but he did it well. It was a way to remind the jury just how sad the death of Rankin was.

This trick made the defense lawyer Durham feel sick. In his mind he saw the picture of Tandy's wife. This frightened little woman had begun crying before the last juror was chosen. She continued to sob throughout most of the afternoon.

When court closed for the day, defense attorney Durham came down the steps. He pushed his way through the crowd. He heard people talking against Tandy, but he said nothing to any of them. What was the use?

After supper at the Drummers' Home Hotel, Durham went up to his room. He found some of the defense team waiting for him. Hightower, the local lawyer who was helping him, was there. And there were also three character witnesses— men from Tandy's home town. They would testify about Tandy's good reputation. These three fellows would be the only witnesses, except Tandy himself, that Durham meant to call.

One of them was a little man named Herman Felsburg. He owned a clothing store. Another was Colonel Quigley, a banker and an ex-mayor. The third was William Pitman Priest. He was a judge who had a court back in Kentucky.

Judge Priest was a big man. He had a voice that was high and whiny, however. The old judge was very well educated, but he sometimes used bad grammar when he spoke. He did it on purpose. It made him seem more like a common man. It was a trick used by many men in Kentucky politics. But there was one thing about the way Judge Priest talked that really stood out. He almost always called men younger than himself "son."

The three witnesses sat at a table. A kerosene lamp cast a soft light around the room. The old judge sat at an open window. He had his white socks on, but his shoes were off. His feet were propped on the window sill. He was smoking a homemade corncob pipe. From the street below came the sound of farm wagons heading home.

Durham sat down in an easy chair. He looked tired. The heart seemed to be gone clean out of him.

"I don't understand these people at all," he said. "We're beating against a stone wall with our bare hands."

Felsburg spoke up. "If it's money that you're needing, Mr. Durham—don't worry. Tandy's father was my very good friend. He helped me when I first came to his town. I'll take care of the money."

"It isn't money, Mr. Felsburg," said Durham. "If I didn't get a cent for my services, I'd still fight this case. I'd do it for the sake of that boy and his poor little wife. But I don't think he'll get a fair trial in this town. They've built up a lot of hate against him. Why, you could cut it off in chunks!"

Then Judge Priest spoke up in his high, reedy voice. "Well, son, I guess maybe you're right. I've been around courthouses for a good many years. And I've learned one important thing. It's a bad sign when the members of a jury look at a prisoner and never at his wife. That's the way it was all day today."

Then Hightower, the local lawyer, spoke up. "Say, Judge Priest. At least I can assure you that the judge in this trial will be fair. He always is. And those jurors are good, solid men. You can't find better men in this county. But they can't *help* being prejudiced. They're only human. There have been bad feelings against Tandy ever since he shot Abner Rankin."

"Tell me something, son. About how many of them jurors would you say are old soldiers?" Judge Priest asked.

"At least four or five that I know of,"

Hightower said. "Maybe more. Almost every man over the age of 50 years old in this part of the country saw service in the Big War."

"Ah, hah," said Judge Priest. "That jury foreman—now he looked like he might have seen some fighting."

"Four years of it," said Hightower. "He was a captain in the cavalry."

"Ah, hah," Judge Priest said again. "Herman," he said to Mr. Felsburg. "Did you notice the fellow who was playing a harmonica in front of the hotel today? He was a tall young black man. I bet he could play almost any tune you asked him to play."

Durham frowned. Why was the judge interested in the skills of a musician at a time like this?

"I wonder if that man is still around," the old judge said, half to himself.

"I saw him just a while ago. He was heading up toward the depot," said Hightower. "There's a train out of here for Memphis at 8:50. It's about 20 minutes of that now."

"Ah, hah—just about," said the judge. "Well, boys," he went on. "We're all going to do the best we can for young Tandy, ain't we?" Then he turned to Durham. "Say, son," he said, "I'd like you to do me a favor."

"What is it?" Durham asked.

"Put me on the stand *last* tomorrow," Judge Priest said. "You wait until you're through with Herman and Colonel Quigley here. Then you call me. I might seem to ramble somewhat in what I say. But, son—you just let me ramble on for a while, will you?"

"Judge Priest, if you think it could possibly do any good, you can ramble all you like," Durham said.

"Much obliged," said the old judge. Then he struggled into his old shoes and stood up. He dusted the ashes from his pipe off his coat. "Herman, have you got any spare cash on you?"

Felsburg nodded and reached into his pocket.

"About ten dollars would be fine," the judge said. "I only brought enough cash to pay my hotel bill. I just want a little extra in case something comes up."

He pocketed his loan and crossed the room. "Boys, I think I'm going to take a little walk before I turn in," he said. "Herman, I may stop by your room a minute as I come back in. The rest of you boys better turn in early and get yourselves a good night's sleep. We'll probably be pretty busy tomorrow."

After he left the room, he put his head back in the door. "Remember, son," he said to Durham. "I may ramble a bit tomorrow."

As the judge headed down the hall, he was whistling a song. The tune was unknown to most of them. But it seemed strangely familiar to Felsburg.

The old judge was still whistling when he stepped outside the hotel. He turned right and headed for the little railroad station at the end of the street.

* * *

In the morning nearly half the town showed up at the trial. Outside the courthouse, the street was empty. The prosecutor had called all his witnesses the day before. Now the defense lawyer lost no time in getting started. As his main witness, Durham called the prisoner to testify in his own behalf.

Young Tandy gave his version of the killing. He spoke honestly. His words would have convinced a fair-minded jury. He said he had gone to Rankin's office in the hope of settling an old argument. Rankin had gotten angry. He had cursed Tandy and made threats on his life. When Rankin pulled out a gun, Tandy pulled out his own. Rankin had pulled his gun first, but Tandy had fired before Rankin could.

That was all there was to it, Tandy said.

Then it was time for the prosecutor, Gilliam, to question Tandy. He went right after him. He took hold like a snapping turtle and hung on like one, too. First, Gilliam made Tandy admit over and over again that he usually carried a pistol. That wasn't such a big thing in Hyattsville. About half the men in town

did. Still, Gilliam made it seem like
Tandy was bloody-minded.

From the look on most of the jurors'
faces, they seemed to believe that
argument.

The questions dragged along for hours.
There was a break for lunch, and then
the trial continued. Gilliam kept at
Tandy all afternoon, trying to twist his
words. But the young man would not be
shaken. He stuck to his story. Twice,
though, he lost his temper. That was just
what Gilliam wanted. It would make the
jury think Tandy couldn't control his
anger.

As for Durham, he had little more to
offer. He called on Mr. Felsburg and
Colonel Quigley. They both said that
Tandy had a good reputation in his home
town. Attorney Gilliam had only a few
questions for those two men. He was in
a hurry for the jury to meet and decide
the case. He figured he had already won.

It was late afternoon when it came
time for Judge Priest to testify.

Durham looked worried. He was

beginning to think that Judge Priest would hurt Tandy's chances. His weight and age caused him to move slowly. He gave the appearance of being a forgetful, long-winded old man. Durham didn't realize that that would make the jurors more sympathetic. They wouldn't see Judge Priest as a stranger—a fancy-speaking outsider. They would think of him as a common man—someone like themselves.

Judge Priest's clothes were old-fashioned. He wore an old black suit and a black string tie. His white shirt was clean, but wrinkled.

After Judge Priest sat down in the witness chair, defense attorney Durham began to question him.

"All right, sir, what is your name?" asked Durham.

"William Pitman Priest."

Even his voice seemed to fit the setting somehow. Its high nasal tone had a kind of small-town feeling to it.

Durham asked the judge a number of questions about his background. The judge made sure to mention that he had been a soldier during the Civil War. Durham asked him which side he had fought for.

"The Southern army," Judge Priest said proudly. "In fact, at one time during the war, I fought in this very town."

He stopped for a moment and smiled at the trial judge. "Sir, I am a judge, like yourself. I know you like to hear witnesses stick to the point. But I have strong memories of the war. I hope you will forgive me if I ramble a bit."

The trial judge had also fought for the South. He asked the prosecutor, "Do you object to this?"

Gilliam didn't think it would hurt his case if Judge Priest rambled. "No, your honor," he said.

"Good," said the judge on the bench. He nodded to Judge Priest. "You may go ahead."

"Well, really, Your Honor, I don't have so very much to say," Judge Priest said. He looked at the jury. "This morning I walked down to a bridge that crosses a little creek in your town. I had been to that bridge during the Big War."

The jurors leaned forward to listen more closely. Suddenly it struck Durham that the old man was putting a kind of spell on them.

"I was here in 1864, serving behind old Bedford Forrest," Judge Priest said.

Aunt Tilly's fan halted in mid-air. General Bedford Forrest was much loved in this town. During the Civil War, he had saved the town from being burned by Northern troops. Judge Priest began talking about the hard times he and his fellow soldiers had been through. As he spoke, the eyes of some jurors grew misty. Then, all of a sudden, Durham interrupted him.

"Judge Priest, do you know the defendant?" he asked. "And if so—how well do you know him?"

"I was just comin' to that," Judge Priest said. "I've known him since he was born. He was a fine boy. And now he's a fine young man. And why not? His father was one of the finest men I ever knew. In fact, he fought beside me here under General Bedford Forrest."

A gasp went up in the courtroom.

Judge Priest continued. "He was wounded right at the edge of that little creek I visited this morning. Just next to the bridge."

Just then Judge Priest pulled at his right ear. Mr. Felsburg was standing next to an open window. He took out a handkerchief and mopped his brow. As he was putting it back, he seemed to wave it like a flag for a moment.

Then the sound of music came drifting in the window. It was the sound of a harmonica playing an old song from the Civil War.

If you want to have a good time,
If you want to have a good time,
If you want to have a good time,
If you want to ride with Bedford—
Join the cavalry!

It was the famous old marching song of General Forrest's troops.

The courtroom was silent as everyone listened. Then the unseen musician moved down Main Street toward the depot and the creek. The song sank lower and lower until it became a thin thread of sound. At last it died out altogether.

Again there was dead silence in the courthouse of Forked Deer County. Nearly everybody was standing up. Many of the jurors and the people in the crowd had tears in their eyes.

Then Aunt Tilly spoke up.

"My dear brother died followin' after General Forrest," she said. Her voice was shaking a little. "I know how I felt then. And I know how this poor little thing must feel now." She rushed over to where the defendant's wife sat.

"There, there, honey," said Aunt Tilly. She put her arm around Tandy's wife. She began mothering the tiny woman as if she were a child. "There now—you just cry on me."

When Aunt Tilly looked up, her eyes were all blurry and wet. Then she waved her fan in the air. "Now, Judge," she said,

"You and those other gentlemen—you can go ahead now."

The prosecutor started to make an objection. But after seeing the looks on the faces in the courtroom, he sat down.

"You may continue, Judge Priest," said the trial judge.

"Thank you kindly, sir, but I was about through anyhow," said Judge Priest. "I just want to add one thing. The Yankees did *not* cross that bridge where the defendant's father was wounded."

Judge Priest got up from the witness chair somewhat stiffly. As he walked by Durham, he whispered, "Son, notice they've quit looking at the defendant. Now they're looking at his wife. It's time to rest your case."

Durham came out of a daze. "Your Honor," he said as he got up, "the defense rests." The judge then ordered the jury to meet. It was time to decide the defendant's fate.

Those jurors were out only six minutes. Their verdict was, "*Not guilty*."

* * *

Walking side by side, Tandy and Durham came down the steps into the soft June night. Tandy took a long, deep breath into his lungs. "Mr. Durham, I owe a great deal to you," he said.

"How's that?" asked Durham.

Just ahead of them, light was shining out a window of the Drummers' Home Hotel. Standing in the street was the figure of old Judge Priest. His face looked a little pink in the lamp light. His voice was high and a bit more reedy than usual. One by one, the judge was counting out coins into the hand of a tall young black man.

"How's that?" asked Durham again.

"I say I owe everything in the world to you," said Tandy.

"No," said Durham. "You owe me the fee you agreed to pay me for defending you. As for owing more—*there's* the man you're looking for."

And he pointed to old Judge Priest.

A Dogged Underdog

Have you ever known someone who just *wouldn't* give in—no matter what the consequences? Singin' Sandy Riggs is just such a man. Read on for some interesting insights into courage and cowardice.

JUDGE PRIEST MADE THE STRANGE STATEMENT THAT
EVERY BRAVE MAN COULD ALSO BE A COWARD.

A Dogged Underdog

My uncle often paid evening visits to old Judge Priest. Sometimes he would bring me with him. Most of the time there would be several other grayheads there, too. In good weather they would sit outside on the porch.

I would sit on the top step of the porch. I'd hug my bare knees together and listen to their stories. It was worth any boy's while to listen to those men.

Squire Rufus Buckley was pretty certain to be there. He was never known to give a straight answer to any question. For fun, people used to try to force him into it. Someone might say to him that it was a fine day.

"Well," the Squire would say, "it is and it ain't. 'Course, it's clear *now*. But you can't tell when it will cloud up."

The Squire owned a little grocery store on the edge of town. On a busy Saturday afternoon, a customer there might say, "Business is pretty good, ain't it Squire?"

"You could say it's good," the Squire would say. "Then again, it's bad. Some things are selling very well. But some things ain't hardly selling at all."

The Squire was no great shakes of a talker. As a listener, though, he was great. He would sit silently for hours as other people talked.

Captain Shelby Woodward could usually be found at Judge Priest's, too. Captain Woodward's specialty was the Civil War—the *Big War*, he called it.

He often liked to tell the story about Miss Em Garrett. When General Grant attacked our town, she saved our flag.

"She hid the flag under her dress," Captain Woodward would say. "Someone told Grant's men that she had the flag. But she wouldn't give it up. She was all alone, but she wasn't scared. The Union soldiers said they'd burn her house down. She still wouldn't give up the flag. Later she took care of the sick and wounded from both sides. Some of the men that had threatened her came to respect her. They'd salute her when she passed by.

"She wore that flag under her skirts for four years," Captain Woodward would say. "And she kept it until she died. Then they buried it with her."

Judge Priest would always say he remembered that story. Then the talk would swing back and forth, each man taking his turn. The stories were mostly about dead people and things that happened long before I was born.

Major J. Q. Pickett was another visitor to Judge Priest's. He was a fancy dresser. He always wore black clothes. And his wife always put a rose in his jacket buttonhole.

Little Herman Felsburg was sure to be there, too. He owned a clothing store.

One night the men were talking about cowardice. Judge Priest made the strange statement that every brave man was a coward. But, he added, every coward could be a brave man, too. It all depended on the time and the place.

That reminded Captain Woodward of another Civil War story. It was about how his brigade tried to hold back General Sherman's Union army.

"Hold him back?" he concluded. "Hah! We were feeding ourselves to him, a bite at a time. But we were doing it to give the rest of the army a chance to fight.

"At the end of four months, we were down from 1,200 men to 240. But we kept on fighting. Now was that bravery? Or was it just pure cowardice? And what is the difference between the two? We didn't have any choice. When you're the underdog, you *have* to fight. There's nothing else for you to do."

Captain Woodward looked up. "Is that true in your experience, Billy?"

"Yes, that's true," said Judge Priest. "I reckon the bravest man that lives is the coward who wants to run, but doesn't. And anyway, the bravest fighters in every war have always been the women. I know it was so in the Big War. The men could go off and get what joy there was out of fighting. The women had no joy at all. They stayed behind and suffered and waited and prayed."

My favorite story-teller of them all was Captain Jasper Lawson. He was 20 years older than any of the other men. He could tie the faded past to the present with great ease. He knew how to make an old story glow again in bright colors.

Captain Jasper was tall, thin, and straight. He stayed that way until he died at 97. It was Captain Jasper who told the story of Singin' Sandy Riggs.

"Speaking of underdogs and things, I remember a story that happened back before you young fellows were born. Back then—in the 1820s and 1830s—carrying a gun wasn't so popular. Men settled their differences with their fists and their feet. And with their teeth, too, sometimes. Oh, yes! There were more teeth knocked out back then than there are now. But there were fewer widows, and not as many orphans.

"This town was a pretty rough place back then. It was *full* of tough people. Remember—this was still the frontier, back in those days.

"The roughest man around was Harve Allen. He was the bully of the county. Harve was more than six feet tall and built like a mountain lion. All the whiskey he'd drunk hadn't burned him out yet. He fought just for the pure love of fighting. Before he'd been here a year, he had a reputation. He'd beaten up half the men in this town. The other half were pretty careful to leave him alone.

"Harve never used anything except his fists—and his feet and his teeth. He never *needed* anything else. So far as anybody knew, he'd never been licked in his whole life. There was nobody to stop him, you see.

"The sheriff lived at the other end of the county. We did have a town constable named Catlett. But he was a skinny little

fellow. Half the grown boys laughed at
Catlett. Harve would just *look* at Catlett
and Catlett would back away. If Harve
was drinking, Catlett would hurry
straight home. He'd pretend he was sick.
He'd stay in bed until Harve finally
stopped beating up people.

"So Harve had things pretty much his
own way. People gave him the whole road
wherever he went. He looked mean
enough for anything. He was long-legged
and raw-boned. His lower lip hung down.
Some people said it was from the weight
of all the swear words he used. His eyes
were as cold as catfish eyes. He wore a
greasy deerskin hunting vest. Most of the
time he went barefoot. The bottoms of
his feet were as rough as sandpaper.

"That's how he looked the first time he
licked Singin' Sandy. And all the other
times, too, for that matter. It was a
Saturday when Harve ran across Singin'
Sandy for the first time. That was always
a busy day in town.

"Now Sandy Riggs was a little man.
He had sandy hair and big gray eyes. His

face was as freckled as a turkey egg. People called him "Singin' Sandy" because he was always humming a tune. It didn't have any words to it, and it really wasn't much of a tune. It sounded more like a big bluebottle fly buzzing than anything else.

"Sandy lived about three miles outside of town. There's a public park there now. But back then it was all deep forest. Sandy had a cub of a boy that looked just like him. The boy was about 14, I reckon. He'd come into town with Sandy the Saturday I'm telling you about.

"Well, some way or other, Singin' Sandy offended Harve Allen. Of course, that wasn't hard to do. Maybe he bumped into him by accident. Anyway, without any warning, Harve knocked him down.

"Sandy lay there on the ground a minute, sort of stunned. Then up he got and made a rush for Harve. He really mixed it up with him for a while.

"Now, a lot of people like to watch fights. But this one was too one-sided to be much fun. In a second Harve had him tripped and thrown. Then he got down on him, hitting him in the face. Singin' Sandy's boy ran in just then. He tried to pull Harve off his dad. Harve stopped pounding Sandy, just for a second. Then, with one backhand, he sent the boy flying. He landed ten feet away.

"The boy bounced right up. He went after Harve again, but some men stopped him. They didn't want to see the little fellow get hurt. Then the boy started crying. But it wasn't a crying from being scared. It was a *mad* crying, if you know what I mean. A couple of men held him until it was over. That wasn't long— about a minute or two. Then Harve Allen got up and backed off, grinning. He always grinned when he'd beaten someone up.

"Some men helped Singin' Sandy to his feet. They poured water over his head and face. He was all bloody and muddy. At first he didn't say a word. Then he got his breath back and wiped some blood off his face. He looked over at Harve Allen, who stood about ten feet away.

Harve was still grinning. Then Sandy said slowly and quietly, 'I'll be back in a month. Wait for me.'

"That was all. Just 'I'll be back in a month' and 'Wait for me.' Then he turned and walked away, his boy by his side. And he started humming that little tune.

"We didn't know then what he'd meant. But we found out. A month later to the day, Singin' Sandy came back to town. Harve Allen was standing in the street in front of a store. Singin' Sandy walked right up to him. 'Well, here I am,' he said. And he went after Harve with his fists.

"Singin' Sandy hit out quick like a cat. But his arms were short. He didn't much more than come up to Harve's shoulder. Even if the punch had landed, it wouldn't have hurt Harve. Sandy was fast, but Harve was faster. Singin' Sandy might have struck like a cat, but Harve could strike like a moccasin snake.

"Again, it was all over almost before it got started.

"Harve Allen yelled just once. Then he knocked Sandy down and kicked him. He kneeled on his chest and hit him in the face. Soon, Singin' Sandy lay still. Then Harve climbed off him and walked away. Nobody dared to give a hand to Singin' Sandy until Harve was gone. But when Harve was out of sight, the men helped Sandy, just like before.

"Singin' Sandy's face looked like it was pounded out of shape. He couldn't get but one eye open. I still remember how that face looked. He held one hand to his side. It turned out that two of his ribs were broken. He took a couple of breaths. Then he looked around for Harve Allen.

"'Tell him something for me,' he said slowly. 'Tell him I'll be back again in a month, the same as usual.'

"Then Singin' Sandy went down the road toward his home. As he walked, he kept falling down and getting up and falling some more. But he kept right on. And believe it or not, he was trying to hum as he went.

"The men watched him until he was out of sight. Then they recalled that Sandy had said just the same words the

last time—that he'd be back in a month.
Two or three men tracked down Harve
Allen and told him that. He swore and
laughed. Then he looked hard at them
and said, 'The little varmint must love a
beating. That's more than I can say for
some other folks around here.'

"The men slipped away fast. They
didn't want Harve to start thinking
they'd sided with Singin' Sandy."

Captain Jasper cleared his throat
briskly. "Well, it went on that way for five
months. And each one of these fights was
just the same. Every month, here would
come Singin' Sandy Riggs, humming to
himself. And every month he was beaten
bad. Then he'd head home. He'd still be
humming—or trying his best to.

"Once Harve beat Sandy up so badly,
they had to put him to bed. He lay there
two days before he could head home. But
he was as tough as swamp hickory.
Before he limped away, he asked for a
favor. He wanted somebody to tell Harve
that he'd be back the next month.

"I guessed there might be two reasons

why Sandy's trips were a month apart.
One reason was that he had an orderly
mind. The other was that it took him a
full month to get over the last beating.

"Anyhow, it went on like that. Sandy
never hurt Harve much to speak of. And
he always got pretty badly hurt himself.
Soon people took to waiting and watching
for the day of the fight. They used to call
it Singin' Sandy's day. The word spread
all up and down the river. Folks would
come from out of the back woods to see
it. But nobody felt the need to interfere.
Some were afraid of Harve Allen. Others
thought Sandy would get tired of the
beatings and quit.

"But they didn't know Sandy very well.

"On the morning of the eighth fight,
Captain Braxton Montjoy was in town.
You may have heard of him. He made a
name for himself during the War of 1812.
Later he became the first mayor of this
here town.

"Captain Montjoy was of fine old stock.
He wasn't afraid of anything that wore
hair or hide. I still remember the little

walking stick he carried. It was made of some kind of shiny black wood. It had a white ivory handle, carved like a woman's leg. And the captain wore his pants strapped down tight under his boots. He was a different sort of fellow.

"That morning he walked over to where Harve was standing. 'Harvey Allen,' he said, 'I think there's a problem. You've been picking on this man Riggs long enough.'

"Harve was big enough to eat Captain Montjoy in two bites. Now he pulled back his lips like a mad dog.

"'What is it to you?' he said.

"'It is a good deal to me,' said Captain Montjoy. 'And it is a good deal to every man who believes in fair play. I'm telling you that I want it stopped.'

"'The man don't walk that can tell me what to do,' said Harve. 'I'm the meanest man in these here parts. I'm half horse, half alligator and I—'

"Captain Montjoy stepped up right close to him. He tapped Harve on the chest with his little walking stick.

"'I don't care to hear about your background,' he said. 'Your family secrets do not concern me, Harvey Allen. What *does* concern me is this: You must stop picking on a man half your size. Do I make my meaning clear?'

"At that, Harve changed his tune. A whine actually came into his voice.

"'Well, why don't he keep away from me then?' he said. 'Why don't he leave me be? Why does he come 'round here every month? Why don't he just quit?'

"Captain Montjoy started to say something more. But just then somebody spoke up behind him. When the captain spun around, there was Singin' Sandy.

"'Excuse me, sir,' he said to Captain Montjoy, 'I'm grateful to you. But this is a private matter. It's got to be settled between me and that man. And there's only just one way to settle it.'

"'Well, sir, how long do you expect to keep this up?' asked Captain Montjoy.

"'Until I lick him,' Singin' Sandy said. 'Until I lick him proper and make him yell for mercy.'

"'Why, you little runt! You ain't *never* going to lick me,' cried Harve. Then he cursed at Sandy. But I noticed he didn't rush him as he usually did. Maybe that was because of Captain Montjoy standing in his way.

"'You're *never* going to be man enough to lick me,' said Harve again.

"'I plan to keep on trying,' said Singin' Sandy. 'And if I don't do it, there's my son. Some day *he'll* do it.'

"Sandy wasn't boasting or arguing. He was simply saying something that was already settled in his mind.

"Captain Montjoy stepped back. He looked straight at Singin' Sandy. There was a purple mark under one of Sandy's eyes. It was a bruise left over from last month's fight.

"'By Godfrey,' said Captain Montjoy. 'By Godfrey, sir!' He pulled off his glove. 'Sir,' he said, 'I would be honored to shake your hand.'

"So the captain and Sandy shook hands. Then the captain stepped to one side and bowed to Sandy. A second later

Sandy stepped toward Harve Allen, humming to himself.

"Strangely, for this one time, Harve didn't charge right in. It seemed like he wanted to back away. But Singin' Sandy lunged out and hit him in the face. The blow stung him. That made Harve's brute fighting instinct come roaring back. He struck Sandy with both fists and knocked him down. He licked Singin' Sandy again that day. But he didn't lick him nearly as bad as he usually did.

"When Harve got through, Singin' Sandy got up by himself. That was the first time he'd been able to do so. He stood there a minute, wiping the blood off his face. Then he spit. We saw that two of his front teeth were missing. Sandy put the tip of his tongue in the empty space.

"'In a month,' he said to Harve. Then away he went, humming his tune.

"Well, I watched Harve Allen closely for the next month. I think nearly all the other townspeople did, too. It was a strange thing. He went through the whole month without beating up anybody. Before that, he'd never let a whole month pass without getting into at least one fight.

"When Singin' Sandy's day rolled round again, it was springtime. The river was running high. That morning, part of the riverbank had washed away. A cabin with some women and children inside was washed away with it.

"For the time being everybody forgot about Sandy. No one even saw him coming until he was standing on the riverbank. As usual, he was humming his little song to himself. Somehow his song seemed louder and clearer than ever before.

"Sandy was watching a boat out in the river, about 50 yards from shore. Harve Allen was on it, fighting the current and dodging logs. And he was rowing straight for the *other* side! It was more than two miles across. Harve never looked back once. Singin' Sandy stood and watched him go. He watched until Harve was nothing more than a spot on the water.

"Well, that was the end of it. Singin' Sandy lived out his life and died here. But Harve Allen never showed his face in town again."

Captain Jasper got up slowly, and shook himself. It was a sign that his story was finished. The other men also got up. It was getting late now—time to be getting on home.

"Well, boys, that's all there is to tell," said Captain Jasper. "That's all that I remember, anyhow. Now what do you think? What would have made Harve Allen run away? Why did he run from a man he'd licked eight times before? Would you call it cowardice?"

It was old Squire Buckley who answered. "Well," he said, "perhaps I would."

Then he added, "On the other hand, perhaps I wouldn't."

Thinking About
the Stories

Five Hundred Dollars Reward

1. Good writing always has an effect on the reader. How did you feel when you finished reading this story? Were you surprised, horrified, amused, sad, touched, or inspired? What elements in the story made you feel that way?

2. How important is the background of the story? Is weather a factor in the story? Is there a war going on or some other unusual circumstance? What influence does the background have on the characters' lives?

3. Are there friends or enemies in this story? Who are they? What forces do you think keep the friends together and the enemies apart?

Words and Music

1. Suppose that this story was the first chapter in a book of many chapters. What would happen next?

2. In what town, city, or country does this story take place? Is the location important to the story? Why or why not?

3. Did the story plot change direction at any point? Explain the turning point of the story.

A Dogged Underdog

1. Many stories are meant to teach a lesson of some kind. Is the author trying to make a point in this story? What is it?

2. What period of time is covered in this story—an hour, a week, several years? What role, if any, does time play in the story?

3. Judge Priest is a character who appears in all three of Cobb's stories. What role does he play in each story? Is he always the main character, or is he always the narrator? How do the townsfolk regard him?

LAKE CLASSICS

Great American Short Stories I

Washington Irving, Nathaniel Hawthorne, Mark Twain, Bret Harte, Edgar Allan Poe, Kate Chopin, Willa Cather, Sarah Orne Jewett, Sherwood Anderson, Charles W. Chesnutt

Great American Short Stories II

Herman Melville, Stephen Crane, Ambrose Bierce, Jack London, Edith Wharton, Charlotte Perkins Gilman, Frank R. Stockton, Hamlin Garland, O. Henry, Richard Harding Davis

Great American Short Stories III

Thomas Bailey Aldrich, Irvin S. Cobb, Rebecca Harding Davis, Theodore Dreiser, Alice Dunbar-Nelson, Edna Ferber, Mary Wilkins Freeman, Henry James, Ring Lardner, Wilbur Daniel Steele

Great British and Irish Short Stories

Arthur Conan Doyle, Saki (H. H. Munro), Rudyard Kipling, Katherine Mansfield, Thomas Hardy, E. M. Forster, Robert Louis Stevenson, H. G. Wells, John Galsworthy, James Joyce

Great Short Stories from Around the World

Guy de Maupassant, Anton Chekhov, Leo Tolstoy, Selma Lagerlöf, Alphonse Daudet, Mori Ogwai, Leopoldo Alas, Rabindranath Tagore, Fyodor Dostoevsky, Honoré de Balzac

Cover and Text Designer: Diann Abbott

Library of Congress Catalog Number: 95-76746
ISBN 1-56103-064-3
Printed in the United States of America
1 9 8 7 6 5 4 3 2 1

LAKE CLASSICS

Great American
Short Stories III

[WITHDRAWN]
Irvin S.
COBB

Stories retold by Prescott Hill
Illustrated by James Balkovek

LAKE EDUCATION
Belmont, California